Sonya's FAMILY

BY ELLIOT RILEY

ILLUSTRATED BY
SRIMALIE BASSANI

Rourke
Educational Media
rourkeeducationalmedia.com

Scan for Related Titles
and Teacher Resources

Before & After Reading Activities

Teaching Focus:
Concepts of Print: Have students find capital letters and punctuation in a sentence. Ask students to explain the purpose for using them in a sentence.

Before Reading:

Building Academic Vocabulary and Background Knowledge
Before reading a book, it is important to set the stage for your child or student by using pre-reading strategies. This will help them develop their vocabulary, increase their reading comprehension, and make connections across the curriculum.

1. Read the title and look at the cover. *Let's make predictions about what this book will be about.*
2. Take a picture walk by talking about the pictures/photographs in the book. Implant the vocabulary as you take the picture walk. Be sure to talk about the text features such as headings, the Table of Contents, glossary, bolded words, captions, charts/diagrams, or Index.
3. Have students read the first page of text with you then have students read the remaining text.
4. Strategy Talk – use to assist students while reading.
   - Get your mouth ready
   - Look at the picture
   - Think…does it make sense
   - Think…does it look right
   - Think…does it sound right
   - Chunk it – by looking for a part you know
5. Read it again.

Content Area Vocabulary
Use glossary words in a sentence.

cousins
fort
sneak
weekdays

After Reading:

Comprehension and Extension Activity
After reading the book, work on the following questions with your child or students in order to check their level of reading comprehension and content mastery.

1. *Name three things Sonya and her brothers do together. (Summarize)*
2. *Who does Sonya live with? (Asking Questions)*
3. *How is Sonya's family like yours? How is it different? (Text to self connection)*
4. *What holiday does Sonya's family spend together? (Asking Questions)*

Extension Activity
Make family puppets! Count the members of your family. Gather that number of paper plates. Draw each of your family members' faces on their own plate. Glue a wooden stick to the back of each plate. Put on a family puppet show!

Table of Contents

This is Sonya. On **weekdays**, she lives with her mom.

On weekends, she lives with her dad.

Sonya has two brothers.

One brother is older than Sonya. One is younger.

Play Time

Sonya and her brothers play dress up.

8

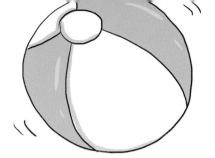

They play ball.

9

They play hide and seek.

"Ready or not, here I come!"

Sonya has three aunts and four uncles.

She has seven **cousins.**

Together Time

Everyone celebrates
Thanksgiving together.

It is Sonya's favorite day.

Sonya and her cousins build a **fort**.

16

Sonya's dad and uncles **sneak** inside.

Sonya's mom and brothers sneak in, too.

"It's squishy in here!"
Sonya giggles.

Sonya loves her family.

Sonya's family loves Sonya.

Picture Glossary

cousins (KUHZ-ins): The children of your uncles or aunts.

fort (fort): A structure that is built to protect people or an area.

sneak (sneek): To move in a quiet, secretive way.

weekdays (WEEK-days): All the days of the week except Saturday and Sunday.

Family Fun

Who are the people in your family?

Draw each person and write their name below their picture.

How is your family portrait like Sonya's? How is it different?

About the Author

Elliot Riley is an author with a big family of her own in Tampa, Florida. She loves when everyone gets together to eat, laugh, and play games. Especially the eating part!

Meet The Author!
www.meetREMauthors.com

Library of Congress PCN Data

Sonya's Family/ Elliot Riley
(All Kinds of Families)
ISBN 978-1-68342-146-7 (hard cover)
ISBN 978-1-68342-188-7 (soft cover)
ISBN 978-1-68342-218-1 (e-Book)
Library of Congress Control Number: 2016956584

Rourke Educational Media
Printed in the United States of America,
North Mankato, Minnesota

www.rourkeeducationalmedia.com

Author Illustration: ©Robert Wicher
Edited by: Keli Sipperley
Cover design and interior design by:
Rhea Magaro-Wallace

Also Available as:

24